LOOK OUT
SAMMY SHARK

This book belongs to . . .

- -

In this story can you find . . .

An octopus?

A stingray?

A turtle?

A pink fish?

A crab?

A starfish

A jellyfish?

A narwhal?

A pufferfish?

A shark called Sammy?

Look Out Sammy Shark

A LAUGHING LOBSTER BOOK 978-1-913906-73-3

Published in Great Britain by Laughing Lobster, an imprint of Centum Publishing Ltd.
This edition published 2023.

3 5 7 9 10 8 6 4 2

Illustrations by Sophie Hanton.

Laughing Lobster, an imprint of Centum Publishing Ltd, 20 Devon Square, Newton Abbot, Devon, TQ12 2HR, UK. 9/10 Fenian St, Dublin 2, D02 RX24, Ireland.

books@centumpublishingltd.co.uk

LAUGHING LOBSTER, CENTUM PUBLISHING LIMITED Reg. No. 08497203

A CIP catalogue record for this book is available from the British Library.

Printed in Great Britain.

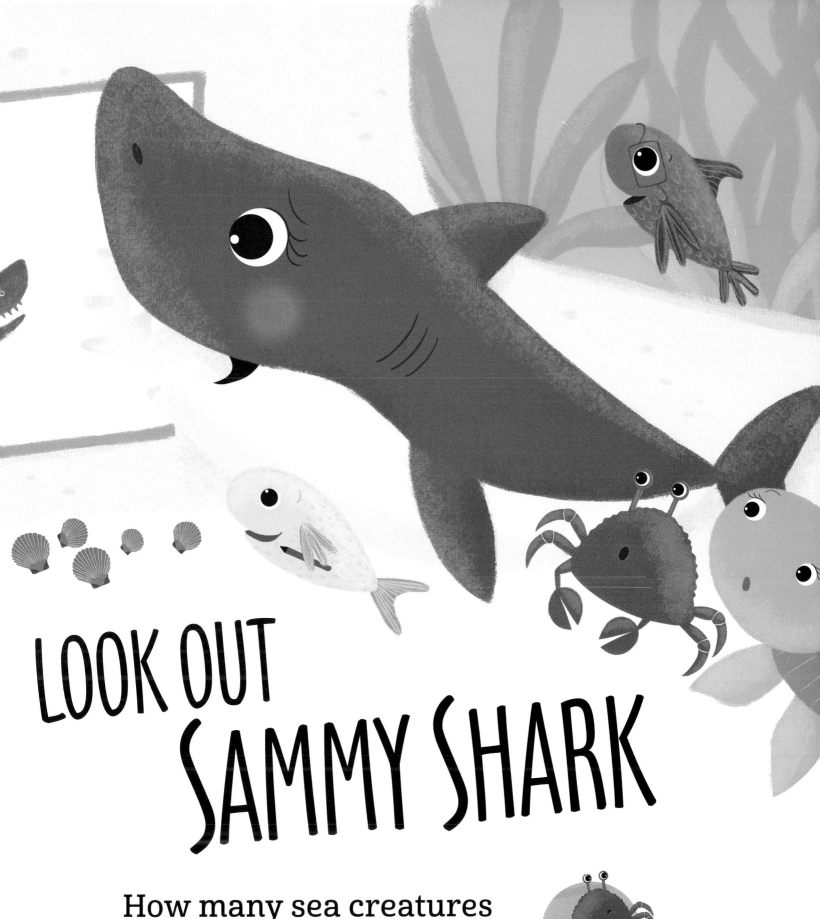

LOOK OUT
SAMMY SHARK

How many sea creatures
can you find on each page?

Sammy the shark can't help chomping things as she rushes around. She always seems to be late!

Sammy is on her way to school. She races for the school bus, but accidentally takes a bite out of it. CHOMP!

At school they all line up ready to go in but Sammy is last off the school bus and rushes to the line. Oh dear, she's knocked into everyone! At least she hasn't chomped anyone this time.

Sammy's so late for class that she rushes to her classroom, speeding into the teacher's desk. GOBBLE!

She's eaten the desk! Whoops!

Lunchtime! Sammy can't wait to sit with her friends, but in her excitement she takes a chunk out of the lunch table. CRUNCH!

MUNCH!

During Maths, when Sammy knows the answer, she zooms up to the board, but can't stop! NIBBLE!

Time for sport and Sammy can't wait to catch the ball, but oh no, it's happened again. GULP!

Everyone is at the start line.
They're all lined up and ready to go.
Will Sammy race past everyone?
Will she accidentally chomp something?

START

Sammy swims so fast she beats everyone else.
She shoots towards the finish and guess
what . . . she doesn't eat the winner's cup!

Sammy is officially the fastest fish in the sea! She has found something that she's really good at. Hooray!

Her teachers are very proud of her and Sammy is delighted. Finally, being fast is a good thing!

Maybe she won't munch things by accident anymore.

Can you remember?

What type of sea creature is Sammy?

How does Sammy get to school?

What does Sammy take a chomp out of in the classroom?

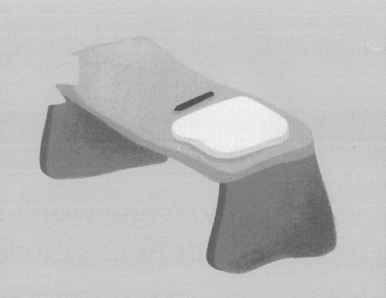

What game do they play in sport?

What does Sammy get for winning the race?

Which teacher gives the winning cup to Sammy?

Did you find?

An octopus?

A stingray?

A turtle?

A pink fish?

A crab?

A starfish

A jellyfish?

A narwhal?

A pufferfish?

A shark called Sammy?